this once upon a time
when i was a rabbit book
belongs to...

once upon a time when i was a rabbit
and there was nothing i couldn't do...

i would leap so high that i would wake
the blue birds and the butterflies sleeping
in the sunlight in the tops of the tall trees,

i would leap so high that the moon

would hide its eyes to

see me coming,

and i would crouch so low that not even

the white owl with the silent wing and

the eagle eye could see me shiver,

and i would crouch so low that not a blade
of grass or a spider's leg could move
the tiniest tiny move without a wink
and a nod from me,

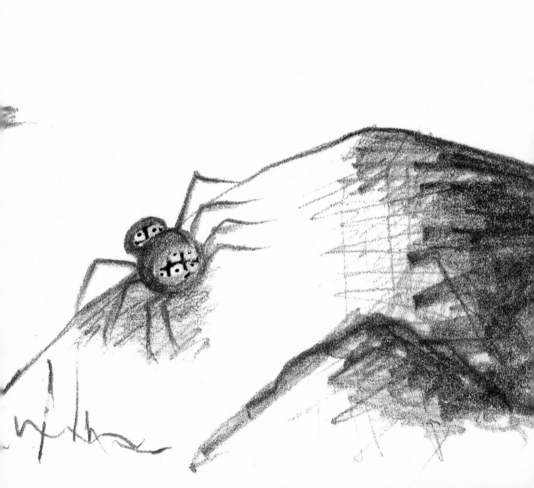

once upon a time when i was a rabbit
and there was nothing i couldn't do...

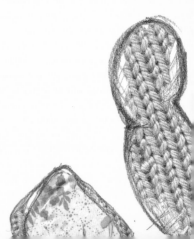

sh**ou**t

i would shout so loud that i would wake
the biggest big bear in the darkest cave
in the high hill,

so that he would stretch and wonder if maybe,
just maybe, there was something bigger out there
in the wide world than the biggest big bear,

and i would whisper so quiet that not one word
of all the most important words that i would
ever say was ever heard at all,

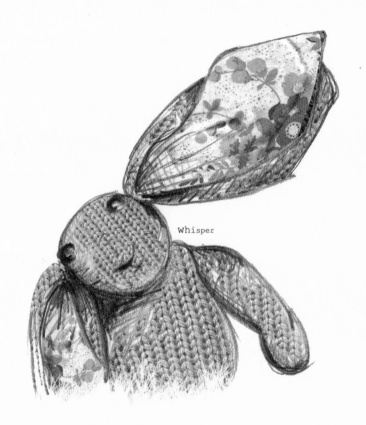

whisper

and i would run so so fast
that the wild wind couldn't catch me
even though he tried and tried and tried and
i slept the day away and gave him a head start,

and i would creep so so slow
that spring would turn to summer
and i would barely have moved between
the grey stone and the willow tree

as the snails went racing by,

once upon a time when i was a rabbit and there was nothing i couldn't do...

i would wait and watch as the sun went down
and i would curl up cosy tight and full of
sound sleepiness to dream my dreams

of once upon a time when i was a rabbit
and there was nothing i couldn't do...

now you've
met the little
rabbit you should
really meet
the biggest big
bear!

Once upon a time

when i was the biggest big bear

in the whole of the wide world...

Printed in Cumbria by Stramongate Press who did a lovely job.

First Printed in 2008

ISBN 9780956096302

temporary measure

The Studio

Braithwaite Farm

Keswick

CA12 5RY

or if that's too far away

you can find us on facebook and twitter

or at www.temporarymeasure.co.uk

or just shout really loud.